Animal Stories by Young Writers

from *Stone Soup* magazine

Edited by

WILLIAM RUBEL AND GERRY MANDEL

TRICYCLE PRESS
Berkeley, California

TRICYCLE PRESS
P.O. Box 7123
Berkeley, California 94707
www.tenspeed.com

Text and cover design by Jeff Puda
The text of this book was set in Granjon

Library of Congress Cataloging-in-Publication Data

Animal stories by young writers / edited by William Rubel and Gerry Mandel.
p. cm.
Summary: An anthology of stories from the magazine "Stone Soup,"
written by children and featuring different types of animals.

ISBN 1-58246-017-5 (paper)
ISBN 1-58246-025-6 (hardcover)

1. Animals—Juvenile fiction. 2. Children's stories, American. 3. Children's
writings, American. [1. Animals—Fiction. 2. Short stories. 3. Children's
writings.] I. Rubel, William. II. Mandel, Gerry.

PZ.A5285 2000

[Fic]—dc21   99-039889

First printing, 2000

Printed in Canada

1 2 3 4 5 6 - 04 03 02 01 00

CONTENTS

EDITORS' INTRODUCTION

This is a book of stories about animals by writers age nine through thirteen selected from *Stone Soup*, the magazine of writing and art by young people. Animals are important in the lives of our writers, which means that stories about animals have been an important part of *Stone Soup* since our first issue twenty-seven years ago.

This book begins with a story about a girl and a wolf—and an intense moment that changes her life—and ends with a poem that puts into words the deep magic that passes between us and our pets. In between these two pieces you will be guided by a ghost dog, become a mouse, find yourself alone with your llama in high mountains in a snowstorm, kill a deer, and become wild like a mustang. You will look into the hearts of animals, and become an animal trying to look into your heart, wondering, "What is that human doing?"

There are animals we love, and animals we fear. There are animals we love that die, and animals we admire that are senselessly killed. There are animals that come into our dreams as spirits of great power, and there are animals of great strength that may need us to save them. There are animals we can only view at a distance and animals we can cuddle with in bed. The eighteen young writers whose works you find here have each succeeded in transforming a thought, a feeling, or an emotion at the core of our experience of animals into stories—or in one case a poem—that are rich with meaning and adventure.

The adventures we meet in stories can be more intense than the adventures we meet in life. The adventure of looking directly into a wolf's eyes and the thrill of knowing what the look means—that is the thrill you find here in the pages of this book. It is the thrill that great literature is able to bring into our lives—the thrill of deep feelings and deep understanding. As editors of *Stone Soup*, we are proud to bring you this collection of stories about animals written by gifted young storytellers.

Loky's Gift

Colleen Flanagan, 12

WITH A SIGH, Calliope leaned back against the rough bark of the tree. She shivered in the cool mountain air and pulled her jacket around her. It's the middle of *June!* she thought unhappily, I shouldn't need a jacket! That was one of the many things that bugged her about this place. But, it had a few good points as well. Such as, it was very serene, and peaceful, away from the smog and noise of the city. *Away from friends.* She frowned. It seemed as if every time she started to have a remotely happy thought, a bad one followed. She blew a wisp of golden-brown hair from her face. She was growing out her bangs, and her hair was in that do-nothing stage. She sighed again. Her binoculars felt heavy on her neck. She picked them up and looked through them.

She could see the whole valley from her perch in the

tree. The valley was mainly dense forest, but near the outer fringes where it sloped upward it was mainly grass. There was a clearing in the middle where a large lake sat. It was great camouflage, and the accessible water supply made it an ideal spot for wildlife. She saw the herd of mountain goats near the edge of the valley, and by the lake she saw the camp. From way up here it was fun to imagine she was just looking at the ground. The pine trees looked like a patch of moss, the lake like a puddle, and the camp looked like a horde of ants, raiding a picnic spot. Calliope smiled. This was the perfect place, on the outer slopes, slanted just enough. She had found this spot last week and sat up here a lot. It was really high up and fairly hard to reach, even for her. She considered herself a natural-born climber. Her father used to call her his little monkey.

Calliope's father was some sort of scientist, or an animal researcher. They were up here observing the gray wolves in the Appalachian Mountains. She really didn't know a lot about what her father did. All she knew was that they did a lot of tagging, tracking, photographing, and recording. Her father had always been gone a lot. Now she saw even less of him, ever since her mother kicked him out two years ago. Her mother complained that he was gone too much. Things didn't really change that much after he had left, but enough for her to notice the difference. She had come up here for the summer because her mother thought she need-ed to spend more time with him. Both she and her father had protested. He argued that this was no place for a child, she'd just get in the way. She argued that there was no way she was going to some God-forsaken rock with no TV, radio, or other kids her age. Her mother argued that there was no way she was going to sit by and watch a perfectly good father-daughter relationship fall apart like theirs did. Her mom won.

Her dad had tried many times since she got there to start a conversation, but she would have none of it. She knew she was being a little hard on him, but there were so many feelings left unresolved. She just couldn't help blaming him for everything. She never understood how he could put some stupid, mangy wolves above his family, and in a way, she didn't want to.

A wolf howl sliced through the air, breaking her train of thought. She looked up, startled to see that it was already getting dark. She slid off the branch and grabbed the tree around the middle, inching down the trunk. The whole process took about ten minutes. When she finally made it down, she looked around. By now, it was so dark she could hardly see her hand in front of her. Oh great. Now I'm really going to catch it. Four or five wolf howls rose up. She shivered. Partly from cold, partly from fear. Even though the wolves had gotten pretty used to them, they were still wild, and unpredictable.

She walked in the direction she thought was camp. It took her about five minutes to realize she was not going in the right direction and about five more to realize that she was lost. A sense of panic rose up inside her, and she ran blindly forward, tearing through the trees and undergrowth. She heard a multitude of howls, closer than before. Now she wished she had paid more attention when her father had been trying to teach her about how each howl, each pitch, meant something different. She hadn't bothered to listen at the time. After all, a howl was a howl was a howl, right? She glanced up at the clear, full moon. It seemed stupid to her that anything would bother howling at it. Did they actually think it would answer? She laughed at herself, despite the situation, then abruptly sobered. She thought she had heard something. Yes! There it was again! It was a splash! She raced forward through the dense trees and burst out through a clearing, where her wild hopes were confirmed! She was at the lake! She knew where she was now, the camp was on the other side. Somehow, she had made a circle. Calliope was suddenly aware of the eerie silence. No howls, no yips, nothing. Silence. *Dead silence.* She heard a twig snap behind her. She froze. She slowly turned around, and her heart dropped to her stomach. To her horror she found herself staring face to face with a wolf! She stood completely still.

"Good doggie, nice wolf. Are you the only one?" she whispered, crouching down on her knees, as if trying to disappear. She wondered which one it was. There were twenty-three in the pack, it was one of the largest in the area. She knew it wasn't Annabus, or Isis, the main breeders, she could easily recognize them. Was it Tefnut? Was it Horace? She scanned her mind for an answer. She thought it was stupid to name the wolves after some dorky Egyptian gods. Even she could have done a better job. She would have named them things like Rocky or Butch. The dark figure stepped toward her and into the moonlight. Now she recognized him! It was Loky, one of the mischievous younger ones. He was always the most curious. He came closer to camp than any of the others. Sometimes Calliope wondered if it was trust or defiance.

Now she stood face to face with him, one of nature's most feared predators. Her father was always saying that

they didn't deserve the bad rap people gave them, now she hoped he was right. She was startled to realize how close he had moved. She could now make out some of his more detailed features. He was all black, with a white stripe down his nose. He had floppy, fuzzy ears and a bushy tail. He had taken the gaunt figure of an adult wolf, but he still had some of his puppy fat. She stood transfixed, as if hypnotized by his intense stare. His eyes were so deep, so soulful, with a hint of sadness, and some playfulness added in. It seemed as if he were scanning her very soul. She now realized why her father was so mesmerized by these majestic beasts. Loky was so close now, she could feel his hot breath on her cheek. Then, she did something totally crazy. She reached out and laid her hand on his neck. She immediately regretted it. That was *really* stupid, Calliope! she scolded herself, now I bet I'm going to lose my hand! But to her amazement, he didn't seem to mind. She ran her hand along his short, bristly coat, and his silky ears. Then, as if the magic snapped, he turned and darted off into the night. She let her hand drop to the ground, but she stood crouched where she was, still savoring the feeling. She didn't know how long she had been there when she felt a gentle hand on her shoulder. She knew it was her father.

"Calliope," he said gently, "come on hon, let's go."

She turned around and looked at her father with new eyes. Suddenly she seemed to understand why he did what he did, and it seemed as if all the years of hatred, when she couldn't understand her father at all, melted away in that moment.

"Did you see it, Dad? Loky! He . . ." she was cut off by her father.

"Yes. I did."

"What was it, Dad? What happened? I feel so different now, like, like something's changed, somehow." She looked up at her father with a renewed childish excitement. He paused a moment before answering.

"Well, I'm not really sure, but I had a similar experience when I was your age, and, well, I guess it changed my life. That was when I knew what I wanted to do with my life. I prefer to think of it as a gift," he said thoughtfully.

"But what does it mean?"

"It means..." he started to say, then paused. "It means whatever you want it to mean." He offered her a hand. Calliope took it and stood up. She hugged her father and followed him back to camp. She knew Loky had given her something she could never return, and she knew that she would never be the same.

Age, Dust, and Animals

Leah Rosenblum, 13

A DRAFT OF COLD AIR WASHES OVER MY BUNK, waking me, and an icy cold dog's nose is pushed into my neck. Dave sings out his good morning welcome. When he leaves I dress, to stand outside, to watch the mist rise and watch things come alive. As I leave the bunkhouse steps I can vaguely see the forms of the powerful horses as they wait impatiently for their breakfast. My feet carry me down the path to the barn, but I'm still not awake. The biting cold hardly touches me as I walk through Stud Barn and absent-mindedly greet the residents. There is no human sound, not even a car, to disturb the peace. Only the cries of the hungry animals. This is my time, the only time I have alone all day, so I keep my wake-up time a secret.

I like to watch the sky lighten; and I like to watch the mist rise. Sitting in the hayloft I smell the barn smell, age, dust, and animals. As I hear the other campers enter the barn I swing down out of the loft, jumping over one stall and dropping into Shemp's stall, my little black-and-white calf friend. This year I am more cautious after last year's fall that strained an arm and bruised a dignity. Slipping quietly over the stall door I join my friends. They don't know that I haven't been with them the whole time.

It is still before six-thirty so we don't talk much, but I move with a machine-like regularity to feed the cow, to lock her in the stanchion, and to milk. When the gray bucket is halfway full, I pat Poppy's sleek side and fill a calf's bottle for Shemp, who still needs milk, not solid food.

Shemp was stepped on when he was first born. He has a bad leg and a stall of his own. Because he is people-shy it took a while for us to become friends, but now he accepts me and loves his morning milk. As I enter the stall he gives a baby moo for his breakfast and I laugh at his funny attempt. It reminds me some of my brother's voice when it was cracking.

My best friend looks over the stall door and the light catches on her blond-brown hair as she swings back and forth on the door. She oohs and ahhs over how cute Shemp is and says she has to feed him tomorrow. But hunger conquers her loyalty and she leaves the two of us alone again. A few minutes later, when Shemp is done, I give him a rub good-bye and wash the nipple and bottle at the hose and set them out to drain. A red racing stud strikes a pose and breathes conceit at me, so I have to go over and talk to him. The walk back down the path is much more interesting than the walk up, and the serenity fills me. Skies like cat eyes arch over the green mountains that protect the small ranch. I walk on slowly, quietly, to drink in the beauty and

perfection. Suddenly I break into an all-out sprint; I had noticed I was all alone and I know that if I'm not in the kitchen soon breakfast is going to be over.

Athena's Gold

Andrea Johnson, 13

C OME ON, GIRL. ONLY A LITTLE FARTHER," murmured Sylvia Addison to the tall, shaggy beast beside her. "Just up to the top."

Athena, a brown-and-white llama, was at the end of a rope held in Sylvia's hand. She grunted disapprovingly.

Sylvia glanced anxiously at the low gray clouds hanging over Vail Valley. It was still early in the fall, but the air was chilly. She hoped to reach the top of this mountain to make a quick sketch before it got too windy and cold. The Addison family ran a small clothing store in the ski-resort town of Vail, Colorado. But the store rarely brought in much money, even in the winter, and Sylvia added a meager sum to their income by painting nature scenes to sell.

Athena pulled impatiently at her halter. She was carrying a pack, which swayed precariously with every rolling step the llama took. She picked her path easily up the forested slope. Sylvia leaned heavily on the llama's woolly side,

breathing hard. After what seemed like hours of steep climbing, they reached the top.

It was a rugged panorama which spread before them. More and higher peaks rose up on every side. Deep green evergreens clung to most of the steep hillsides, but other summits rose above the timberline, bare and stony. Somewhere in this area, Sylvia remembered her father's grandfather had once operated a gold mine.

The girl shivered, but she wasn't cold. The sheer size of the Rocky Mountains made her feel small and helpless. If she could reproduce this wonder on her canvas, people would be willing to pay a price for it. Any money was helpful to the five Addisons—the clothing store was struggling.

Athena followed Sylvia patiently across the rounded, grassy top of the mountain. On command, she kneeled upon the short tufts of grass. Sylvia removed the portable drawing desk from the llama's pack and set it up on the grass. She took out paper and pencils. She would have taken a photo of the huge granite peak before her to take home and paint, but the camera was broken.

The girl seated herself on the grass. Athena soon had some of the dry stuff in her mouth and was chewing in the llama's odd, sideways fashion. Sylvia hurried, sketching the crags and ridges.

Athena wandered away, the lead rope trailing behind her in the grass. She meandered over the hilltop and, for reasons best known to herself, decided to relax beside a stony cliff that dropped hundreds of feet to jagged boulders and slopes of gravel. A biting wind rose, sending the clouds scudding darkly across the sky. Athena turned her face away from the wind. The thick, fleecy wool protected her from the wind pretty well.

Sylvia looked up from her drawing, watching Athena's small head turn this way and that on her long neck. The temperature was dropping rapidly, but the girl did not want to go home. Things would not be pleasant there...everyone was upset when money ran low. Her two sisters would quarrel, her parents would be irritable. She just had to get something good down on the paper to paint when she returned! She put on her heavy coat and zipped it.

Sylvia leaned back. The coat was warm and comfortable, and she was so tired after working late last night at the store. Her eyes closed, shutting out the darkening sky, and she heard Athena walk near. The llama kneeled beside her and her methodical chewing started. The wind whistled over the rough ground on the exposed mountaintop, but Sylvia did not hear it. She was asleep.

Sylvia was cold. Everything was wet, rough, and icy. She awoke slowly, floating upward through the mists of unconsciousness into the chill. Her eyes opened.

There was snow all around, drifting over her legs and resting in a light powder on her head. She shook the snow out of her hair and sat up. Athena had moved a little distance away and was huddled in the shelter of a big rock. Snow was dusted into her thick wool, but she was awake and alert. The llama made a grunting, whistling sound when her mistress moved. Looking around, Sylvia realized that she had been sleeping for a long time. The snow had stopped falling for a time, but it soon became apparent that this was only a lull in the storm, as the wind picked up again and white crystals began to swirl thickly through the air. Her paper had blown away and the desk was tipped over. Awkwardly, she carried the desk over to the rock where Athena was and curled up with her llama. Sylvia summed up her situation.

It was almost completely dark, which she knew was partly due to the clouds and the snow, but which also meant that it was much later than she had planned to be back. And this meant a couple of very worried parents. But her parents were not there, and she was on the top of a mountain with only her llama for company. To top things off, it was snowing. Hard.

The girl decided that the only thing she could do was to rest and wait for somebody to come. She knew that she could freeze to death in very cold weather unless she moved around. But she was not dressed to hike through the snow. It would soak through her jeans and make her even more freezing than she already was. At least she could eat the lunch she had packed on Athena while she was waiting for her father to find her.

Turning to the much-whitened llama, she fumbled with the straps to remove the whole pack. After she had taken it off, she realized that the food was gone.

It had fallen out somewhere along the way! But no, she had seen it when she removed her paper and the fold-up desk. So it must have slid out of the pack while Athena was wandering around the slope. Annoyed, the girl felt in the snow all around the llama. All she ended up with was a handful of frosty grass and extremely cold hands. She tried to remember where Athena had been.

Oh, yes! It would be at the edge of the cliff, because that was where Athena had lain down. If the pack had not been fastened securely, things would fall out most easily when the llama was kneeling. So Sylvia set out to reach the cliff, being very careful, of course, not to fall off the edge, and retrieve her food.

Athena watched her go with mild interest. Humans

were always going off on their own little errands, which very rarely made any sense and almost never produced a carrot. Athena loved carrots.

But the girl was not returning. Athena was very patient. The cold was not intolerable, and her instincts told her to wait out the storm. But...well, once in a very great while a human errand did turn up a carrot or two.

So the llama walked slowly through the whirling whiteness, following the direction in which she knew the girl had gone. She sensed the drop before she reached it and stepped cautiously to the edge of the cliff. The girl was down there, and she was making noises.

"Athena!" cried Sylvia. She was crying and her voice shook. She could barely make out the dark shape of the llama above her. The package with her lunch in it was on the very edge of the cliff...she had reached for it, and slipped. It was not surprising. One should not lean over the edge of a cliff in a blinding snowstorm. She had caught on a very narrow ledge just below the food.

Sylvia knew that she was lucky. Of course, if the hero of a novel or a movie falls off a cliff, that person will land on a ledge, or maybe grab a tree root. But she would never have dreamed that fourteen-year-old Sylvia Addison, who was not a movie star, or anything even remotely exciting, would have such remarkable luck.

She felt mist that was not snow falling onto her face as Athena spit worriedly. "Athena, go home!" she cried helplessly. "You've got to go back and get somebody!" She was barely hanging on; the frequent blasts of freezing air that blew over the mountain were strong, and bitter with bone-numbing cold.

The llama had not the faintest idea what Sylvia wanted

her to do. But her voice sounded as though she was giving a command. The llama dropped to her knobby knees, rose again, and spit confusedly into the wind. She tramped nervously about on the edge of the cliff. Her prancing hoof dislodged the sack of food and it fell. Sylvia saw it and reached hopefully upward, but it slid coldly through her grasp and fell into the dark abyss below.

Sylvia gave up. She slumped over, knowing that the llama could not help her, and cried.

Athena knew that something was wrong with Sylvia. The llama did not return to her home; she didn't know to attract attention to the girl, and besides, she had had bad experiences when she wandered away from Sylvia before. She had no desire to merge with crowds of excitable, noisy humans ever again. So she settled down to wait out the storm and the icy, gusting wind, and kneeled at the edge of the cliff. Her lead rope fell down to the ledge below.

It struck Sylvia. She looked up and saw the rope. Not realizing that it was Athena's rope, she grabbed onto it and started to pull herself up. Her feet scraped on the stone and sent a large rock, along with most of the ledge, rattling into the canyon.

Athena felt the weight on her halter. She leaned forward, trying to follow the rope as she had been trained to do. But it kept pulling, and the weight grew. The llama gave a short, blasting snort and leaned back against the pull on her halter. Soon she was standing up and pulling back with all her might. And, suddenly, the girl's pale, frostbitten face came up over the ledge. Her feet were on the solid ground and she released the rope, crawling away from the edge before she stood up. Athena pulled back in relief and walked away, spitting and snorting indignantly. Sylvia followed and put her arm around the llama, leaning on her heavily for support.

A large shadow, darker than the trees, emerged from the forest, and a beam of light sliced through the darkness. Sylvia drew back in alarm, shielding herself with Athena's hard, shaggy body. "Who's there?" she asked in a quavering voice, and wished frantically that their Doberman was with her, as he usually was.

"It's me, Sylvia!" came her father's reassuring voice. Athena stood aside, with a look of obvious disgust on her long face, while the two humans embraced each other and talked briefly. Humans did strange things like that. The girl was talking excitedly and pointing at Athena. The man shook his head and walked to the edge of the cliff. He looked down.

Sylvia watched as her father observed the place where she had fallen. She watched his face change suddenly from anxiety to amazement, disbelief, and then excitement.

"Sylvia!" he cried joyfully. "It's gold!" She peeked over with her father holding onto her. The flashlight illuminated glittering minerals inside a hole which her kicking feet had opened up. "But Dad, how can you be sure?" she asked. It was too good to be true.

"No, it is gold! My father told me about a vein right in this area. His father was trying to mine it and found it very pure, but one night when nobody was there the whole thing caved in, and they were never able to locate the exact site again. That's why those tailings are at the bottom of the canyon!" He pointed, but the flashlight wasn't powerful enough to reach the bottom of the chasm. "We've found my grandfather's mine!" He danced around the hill. "We're rich! All we have to do is get it out. It may be tough, but we'll do it."

"But, Dad," said the girl quietly, "it's really Athena that discovered it. If she hadn't happened to lower her rope, I wouldn't have been saved until you came...." Sylvia reflected that she might not have been saved at all, unless her father had happened to look over the edge of the cliff; Sylvia would not have known her father was there, for the wind was blowing hard and it was difficult to hear. But she said nothing of this. It was too terrible to talk about. "Good old Athena."

"I know," answered Mr. Addison slowly. "I know."

And Athena looked on, calm and uncomprehending. She uttered a short bleat and looked surprised when the two people laughed.

The Captive

Nicholaus Curby, 12

WILL TURNER SCRAMBLED DOWN the mountain trail from his house to the valley. He couldn't be late for his first real job!

Although early morning mist half hid the valley, he could see the big sign that marked his destination:

SAM'S SERVICE STATION:

FAST FOOD AND FUEL

Then Will saw something move outside the building. It looks like an animal inside a cage, Will thought, as he started to run. But investigating had to wait. Sam Dickson was standing at the station door.

"Hello. I'm glad you're here!" Will's new employer tapped the walking cast on his left leg. "This broken ankle makes working hard. I can use your help."

The morning was busy. Pumping gas, wiping windshields, fetching soda pop, Will forgot the movement he had seen in the fog until eleven o'clock. Then he ran around the building. In a cage, a large eagle ruffled his bronze feathers and cocked his head as Will approached.

Mr. Dickson hobbled up. "Isn't he a beauty? Found him hurt, but he's well now."

"First one I've ever seen," Will said.

"How'd you like to take over feeding him?"

"Yes sir! But keeping an eagle, isn't it against the law? Why don't you let him go?"

"Let him go!" Mr. Dickson echoed. "Why, I saved his life, besides, I like him."

Later, Will carried out a tray of meat scraps. He slid it into the cage. "Here, old fellow."

The eagle's strong beak tore the meat scraps, and soon the tray was empty. Will stared uncomfortably as the bird pushed fiercely against the cage. "If you were free," Will declared, "you could find your own dinner."

Will loved his new job. Only one thing bothered him— the eagle. Somehow it seemed wrong for such a splendid creature to be trapped.

"I've been reading about wild birds," Will said one afternoon when Mr. Dickson was resting his leg. "Did you know eagles keep the same nest year after year?" He glanced at his employer. "Bet your eagle's thinking about his home right now."

"Nonsense," Sam Dickson said sharply. "That bird has a good home right here."

"I guess so," Will murmured, afraid to say any more.

When Will arrived early the next morning, heavy clouds were gathering overhead. He knew they signaled a big storm. "Maybe you should go tomorrow for supplies," he said to Mr. Dickson, who was writing a list.

"Nope, I always go on Tuesdays. Don't worry, son. I'll be fine." Sam Dickson climbed awkwardly into his red pick-up truck.

"Remember to buy ketchup," Will called as the truck pulled away. Before it disappeared, thunder sounded, and a downpour began.

Only one customer appeared all morning. "Roads are bad," the driver declared. "Hope the rain stops before we have a mudslide."

By noon Will was worried. Mr. Dickson should have been back by this time.

"I'll call the town," he said. He picked up the telephone; it was dead. "The lines are down! I'd better look for him."

Pulling on his slicker, Will walked along the deserted rain-washed road. He wondered where the cars were. He started to run, turned a bend in the road...then he saw it—a great pile of rocks, upside-down trees, twisted roots holding chunks of earth.

"A mudslide, the road is blocked! What if Mr. Dickson was coming back and..."

Slipping and struggling, Will climbed on a huge rock and began to shout. "Mr. Dickson!" His eyes searched the jumble of mud, rocks, and branches. He shouted again, "Mr. Dickson, Mr...."

Wait! Was that a patch of red? The truck? Will pushed his way through the broken trees until he was certain.

Moments later, hands and face scratched, he reached the truck. It lay on its side, pinned down on its side by a giant tree, and the exposed door was smashed in. Will could hear Mr. Dickson pounding and yelling.

"I'm trapped," Mr. Dickson cried, "get me out, Will." Will tugged at the buckled door.

"It won't budge," he shouted. "I'll get help."

It was a long trip to town, but Will ran all the way. When he stumbled into the sheriff's office, he was so breathless he couldn't speak.

"Trapped!" exclaimed Sheriff Jones when Will finally made himself understood. He grabbed a first-aid kit and a crowbar. "Let's go, kid!"

Bouncing along in the sheriff's jeep, Will pointed the way to the red truck. The two jumped out, yelling as they scrambled through the trees and branches.

"We're here, Mr. Dickson!"

"Hang on, Sam!"

They wedged the crowbar between the truck body and the buckled door. They took a firm hold on the handle. "Pull, Will! Hard!" The door didn't move. "Harder."

With a loud crunching noise the door broke open. Will and the sheriff half-dragged the frightened man from the truck. Then the three drove along the roads to the service station.

Will helped Mr. Dickson into the station and started toward the kitchen. "You need some hot soup."

"Wait, Will. Open the cash register. You deserve a reward."

Will hesitated. "I don't want money, but there is something..."

Mr. Dickson stared at Will. "The eagle?"

Will nodded.

"You want to turn him loose, don't you?"

"Yes, sir."

Sam Dickson half smiled. "I do too. I know how it feels to be trapped. Go ahead, open the cage."

Outside the rain had stopped. Will unlatched the cage

door and swung it open. The eagle gazed solemnly at the man and the boy. Then he stepped out onto the platform.

Suddenly he sprang! Strong wings spread wide, then beat more and more powerfully to lift him to freedom. The eagle, no longer captive, soared into the afternoon sky.

Licorice and Me

Heather Sarles, 12

I SURE AM GOING TO MISS YOU, LICORICE!" I said to myself as crystal-blue tears welled up in my eyes and spilled down my face. The warm dirt felt good as I sifted it through my fingers and patted it on the grave mound. It was a warm spring morning and my pet skunk had died after I had had her for five years. I thought back to how I first got her and the memorable and hilarious times we had together.

It was a typical cool, windy spring afternoon in Wyoming when my dad came from checking the traps. I was sitting on the porch swing reading *The Dollhouse Murders* and drinking fragrant apple juice.

"Heather? Heather! Come here for a second. I have a surprise for you."

"Oh, goody! What is it?" I asked, delighted.

"I stopped to check the box trap near the chicken coop.

I found a mother skunk and this one had babies in the box trap. I had to shoot the others, but I brought the runt home for you to keep for a while. Then we will have to shoot it, too, because skunks are predators and they'll kill our poultry."

"But, Dad, you can't just kill an animal if it does something wrong," I cried out plaintively.

"Now, Heather, no arguing. You know that as a rancher I have to do what's necessary," Dad said, raising his voice. "Predators have to be killed or they will multiply and interfere with the way we make our living."

"Dad, you have to realize animals need to survive by getting food, too. You just don't kill them because they get food to meet their basic needs in the only way they know!" I protested.

"Heather, I must warn you that eventually your skunk might be destroyed, if she causes trouble. Skunks are predators and must be disposed of," Dad said warningly.

So I knew I had to raise a well-mannered, well-behaved pet skunk!

Dad had brought home the runt of the litter. It looked like it needed love and care. I named her Licorice because it was my favorite candy and she looked like licorice candy. She was probably a day or two old. She had two stripes on each side and they met at the tail. She looked like a little butterball all curled up. She cried a lot because she was hungry, cold, and lonesome. I warmed some milk and fed her with an eyedropper. I wrapped her in a towel and put her in a wicker basket in my room. I put a ticking clock in the basket to keep her company because she was accustomed to hearing her mother's heart beating when she was in the uterus.

Licorice seemed to develop well on the milk and she

grew and thrived. Five weeks passed before her eyes opened. We took her to the vet and had her de-scented. She had beautiful deep brown eyes that were almost black. She was the cutest thing I ever saw! She waddled around the house walking like a person whose shoes were too tight! She was fastidious like a cat and licked and groomed herself. As she grew older, she ate insects, mice, gophers, reptiles, squirrels, eggs, and people's poultry. She also ate table scraps. Skunks are helpful to farmers and ranchers by killing pests.

Licorice slept in my room. Each night I rocked her to sleep and tucked her in her basket beside my bed.

It took a while for my family to adapt and learn to love Licorice, but they got used to her eventually and learned to love her, too. When company came, we usually had to put her in my room because they were scared of her. People have bad attitudes toward skunks because of the smell of wild ones, and because skunks are predators and will kill chickens, turkeys, and ducks.

Licorice was a great companion. I taught her some tricks like rolling over, playing dead, and clapping. When Dad, Mom, Erin, and I watched TV, if Licorice saw something she liked, she would stand on her back legs and clap. I would tie a red ribbon in her black-and-white tail and she'd prance around feeling pretty and proud of herself. Licorice's all-time favorite food was vanilla ice cream with Oreo cookies. But the best times were the ones we spent together. On warm spring afternoons we would play with a purple ball on the velvety lawn grass. When Erin and I went swimming or wading in the creek, Licorice would go along and splash around in the shallow water.

One late spring early Saturday morning, Dad woke me up and said, "Heather, we are going to brand and the family's coming to help. They're here and are getting ready to eat breakfast. Then we'll ride to round up the cattle."

"OK," I replied sleepily. As Licorice and I started downstairs good aromas were drifting up from the kitchen below. When I got to the table, crispy bacon, fresh-squeezed orange juice, over-easy eggs, toasted, cream-cheese-covered bagels, and home-baked bread with fresh raspberry jam were sitting on the oval oak table.

After breakfast we went out to the barn to get our horses. I tethered Licorice up in the front yard because I was not sure how our livestock would react to her and if she would do anything to spook the horses.

Dad said, "Maybe your horse, Tonto, would let Licorice sit in the saddle with you."

"That's OK, Dad, Licorice needs to learn she can't go everywhere with me," I replied.

We started out to gather the cattle, and within an hour we had them in the corral, ready for branding. I went to the yard to check on Licorice, and when I went around the corner there was muddy dirt all over the lawn. Licorice, a handy digger, had torn up my mom's most precious flower garden that included a rose plant from my Uncle Roger who had died. My mom was standing over Licorice, shaking her finger and admonishing her to lie down. I was shocked to see what Licorice had done because she had never done such a thing before. She had behaved so well in the four years we had her.

Before we started the actual branding I tied Licorice up, this time in a stall in the barn where she couldn't get into trouble. My job during the branding was to help run the vaccine gun. As the calves came through the chute I gave them five cc's of vaccine. We had 450 pretty big calves to do. We had 100 done when my mom came to tell us it was lunchtime. I decided to check on Licorice. When I got to the stall, she wasn't on her tether. She had chewed through it and gotten away. I looked everywhere for her, but I couldn't find her.

Then I realized she was probably in the chicken coop because she liked to eat eggs. I ran there as fast as I could, threw open the door, and there she was with three of our best laying hens dead! She was getting bigger and older, and it is natural for skunks to eat poultry.

Then I heard Dad call my name.

When I heard his voice I wanted to sink into the floor because I figured he wanted to talk to me about Licorice. I didn't want my parents to find out about Licorice's misdeeds in the chicken house, but when he walked in the door of the chicken coop, I knew from the look on his face Licorice and I were in big trouble.

"What is this?" he asked, holding up the three dead chickens.

I slunk back into the corner and replied, "Licorice got loose and found her way to the chicken coop."

"Heather, this is it!" he said, raising his voice. "Licorice has to go, now! She is behaving like polecats behave, and we can no longer keep her!"

"Give her one more chance, please!" I pleaded.

"No, tomorrow morning I will have to destroy her!" he replied quickly.

"Please, Dad!" I cried, choking back tears.

"For now, please go put her in your room so we can finish branding."

As we walked back to the house, I felt like running away and crying my heart out! But I had no time for that with branding, so I did what I was told.

After we were done branding, I took Licorice down to the creek with me. We splashed around and played with her purple ball. Then we ate vanilla ice cream with Oreo cookies. As we ate I talked to her and she stared at me with wondering eyes. I could not believe what was going to happen to my beloved skunk!

That night when I went to bed I cried myself to sleep. I had left my door open by accident. After I was asleep, Licorice apparently slipped out of the house. She wandered across the field and got into the neighbors' yard. Later that night I heard a shot ring out in the night. I sat straight up in bed and looked in Licorice's basket, but she wasn't there.

I ran downstairs and woke up Mom and Dad. Dad said, "We will check in the morning." I went back upstairs to bed, worrying that Licorice might be in trouble.

When I woke up, the smells of crispy bacon and eggs were drifting into my room. When I went down to breakfast, Dad said, "Heather, Licorice is dead. She got into the neighbors' chickens last night, and they shot her. They did not realize she was your pet, thinking she was a wild predator."

"Oh, no!" I cried.

"Yes," said Dad, "she is wrapped in a sheet on the porch. You may bury her this morning."

"Yes, Father, I will do it," I said sadly, my worst fears come true. I got a doll box and lined it with a blanket from her basket where she slept by my bed. I went out and climbed the hill overlooking Rock Creek. I dug a hole with a shovel, turning over the moist red-brown soil, and put her in. I said some words over her and shoveled the dirt back into the grave. I dug; then I patted the topsoil over her. I picked some wild prairie flowers—bluebells, buttercups, and shooting stars—and put them on her grave.

"I will never forget you, Licorice." I turned and walked away into the morning light, moving slowly and heavily.

Coon Wolves

Kathi Hudson, 12

I COULD SEE THE SNOWFLAKES falling outside my window. The windows frosted up as the cold from outdoors met the warmth of my living room. It was so nice to sit by the fireplace in the house my father had built long ago. Everything was perfect. I had my two best friends, Ruff and Snowy, with me. They are old wolves now, but I can picture the day I found them as clearly as I could the next day. I love memories and this one is especially dear to me.

I was a young boy of just ten then. We lived in the same house that I live in now. I loved the Ozarks. They were my mountains as far as I was concerned. I was somewhat of a loner. Oh, sure, I had friends, but no one that I was really close to. I needed someone, or something.

There wasn't much to do in those days, except eat, sleep, and go to school. The days were boring unless, by some wonderful chance, you had a dog. Not just any dog either, it had to be a coon dog. I was determined that if I had one at all, he had to be the best.

Whenever I heard of someone's coon dog having, or being the father of, pups, I would go check 'em out. I never really did find any good ones that had a price within reason. Just once; it was Sam Owens's dog. He and his dog were the best coon hunters in the whole county. As soon as I heard the news, I ran to see the pups. They all looked pretty shabby except one. He was brown, all brown, except one spot of white on the tip of his left ear. I hoped and prayed, as I walked over to Sam, that the price would be right. That pup had all the markings of a good hunter.

Sam said, "Well, son, I was going to sell him for 'bout thirty bucks." As my eyes fell he said, "But for you, I'll let him go at twenty." My face brightened. Twenty dollars was still a lot of money for a ten-year-old boy, but for that dog, nothing was impossible. For the following weeks, I worked, I worked ever so hard. Finally I had the money. I took it to the Owens's. I wished all the way there that the dog was still there.

When I got to the ranch, I gave Sam the money. His eyes fell as he spoke. "I'm so sorry," he said, "I didn't think you had the money. I waited so long. I'm sorry. Sold 'im yesterday to a feller down the street. I'm so sorry!" he said with tears in his eyes.

I had never felt so low in my life. My dog, gone. The tears stung in my eyes as I ran away, without another word. I ran all the way home. I burst into the kitchen of my house. "Tom! Can I see your dog?" my ma yelled after me.

"Ain't one to see!" I yelled back, still running, choking on my tears. I cried all night, and all the next day. That sounds very unrealistic, but it's true. So true.

By the next week I had decided that the world had not stopped and I must go on without my pup.

One day, I was walking through the forest, one of my favorite things to do. I felt tired so I lay down in the soft pine needles and fell asleep. I awoke with a start. There was a sound of crying. I looked around. It seemed to be coming from behind a log. I looked. There they were, two baby wolves, cold, hungry and deserted. I looked around. I found their mother, lying in some nearby bushes, dead. The cause of her death? I don't know. Probably never will. All I know is that when I saw those pups, my world turned bright again. I knew they needed someone, and that someone would be me. As I carried them home, running through the fields with one in each arm, I knew my ma and pa would let me keep them. They would hunt better than dogs because they are wild. They would be the best coon wolves in the whole country! The thoughts flowed: training them, hunting, having not one but two best friends!

The Doe

Daniel Whang, 12

THE FREEZING MORNING BREEZE tingled against my face as I stepped out on the balcony and inhaled the fresh air. It was Christmas morning and I was excited about the events that were going to take place that afternoon. I wasn't excited because of the presents or the Christmas dinner but because today I would go on my first hunting trip at the nearby Catalina mountains. I looked out at the mountains, wondering which deer under the cream-topped forest would be mine. My moment of silence was interrupted when a deafening CRACK, followed by a triumphant "HEEHAH! I got 'im!" echoed in the mountains. I wasn't alarmed at the sound; the Catalinas had a reputation for having trophy-sized deer, and many hunters, including my father and my brother Paul, hunted there. Soon, I would join their club.

"Peter! Get ready, we're going soon!"

I nearly jumped at my brother's booming voice. I ran back inside. Then I headed to my room.

When I got back to my room, Dad and Paul were there to greet me.

"It's initiation time." My dad looked at me with beaming eyes and a glowing smile. "Come here, son." I went over and my dad handed me a white and blazing-orange coat. "Like it?" he asked.

I tried it on, then I looked at myself in my full-length mirror. I didn't look half bad in it. "It's great. Thanks."

"Don't thank me, thank your brother. He got it for you as a present."

"Thanks, Paul," I said.

"Ho, ho, ho!" he answered.

"OK, men. Let's get ready." My dad sounded like an army lieutenant getting ready for battle.

After they left my room, I put on my coat and grabbed a bag which contained my shotgun. I ran downstairs and waited on the sofa.

When they came down, we all left the house one behind the other, my dad leading, of course. We threw our guns in the back of the pickup truck and sped off to the mountains.

On our way up the mountain, I saw two hunters on the side of the road loading two deer in their truck. The deer were almost unrecognizable because they were drenched in their own blood. I began to feel sorry for the deer, but I discarded the thought by saying to myself, "I can't think this way. I'm a hunter." I slept the rest of the way there.

I was awakened by the happy voice of my father saying, "OK, time to hunt the big game."

I got out of the truck full of excitement. We all grabbed our rifles. Dad made Paul and me carry the stretcher which we used to transport the deer.

When we got to a place where the forest met a small clearing, we stopped. We waited for half an hour until a large doe, unaware of the dangers waiting for her, wandered into the clearing. Dad motioned to me to take the shot.

I felt butterflies in my stomach as I picked up my shotgun. The cold metal stuck to my hands, but I ignored it. I brought the gun up to my face until I could clearly see the deer through the sights, while my father chanted away, "Make the first shot count." I watched the deer peacefully pushing the snow away from the buried grass. I placed my finger on the trigger. I began to think about what I was doing. I was killing an innocent life practically for fun. Then I began to think, It's legal, and plus, my family is depending on me to bring the pot home. But I made my decision, I wouldn't shoot. Meanwhile, Paul and Dad were practically going nuts because I wasn't doing anything.

I kept hearing, "Hurry up and kill it, before I do."

I felt pressure. Too much pressure. I was too mixed up. I was beginning to fall into the hands of my family.

BOOM! I felt a shock run through my body. I stared disbelieving at the doe which was struggling to stay alive, looking at me as if I had betrayed her. I gazed at the smoking gun and then at my finger which betrayed me. I refused to believe that I shot the doe. I wanted to scream, but when I opened my mouth nothing came out. I ran over to the dead deer, and when I saw the bullet hole which was surrounded by blood I vomited.

My dad asked me if I was all right. I didn't answer. Then he told Paul to put the deer in the stretcher.

I ran back to the truck and sat motionless, still unable to get over what had just happened.

When we finally left, I vowed to myself that I would never shoot a gun again.

Night Predators

Jessica Limbacher, 10

"Hoo-hoo-hoooooo."

He could hear the eerie sounds of a horned owl as he tried to sleep. To the little squirrel, owls were an oddity. Such big tufts on their heads. And huge eyes as big as walnuts that searched along the forest floor. And strangest of all, their long, low hoot.

The squirrel closed his eyes and tried to sleep. But the once-comforting sound of the rushing crystalline water now kept him awake. He did not feel safe, even though he was covered by a blanket of darkness as black as ink.

He looked up into the dark sky. The clouds obscured the opal-like moon. An invigorating breeze whistled through the branches, which made a most unpalatable thumping noise.

The little squirrel began to get restless, so he crept down his tree and took a sip of the cool water in the creek.

Eerie sounds of night creatures paralyzed the squirrel and he stood frozen like a statue. He wanted to scurry up his big oak tree, but his legs refused. Then he heard a stick crack that broke the silence like glass shattering and saw pale yellow eyes, those of a fox. Now his legs snapped into action and he darted as fast as the wind, this way and that, trying to find his tree. The squirrel's heart pounded wildly in his chest as he ran. The formidable fox was close behind. As the squirrel glanced behind him, he could see the fox's treacle-colored fur turn black and blend in with the dark night.

Suddenly, the fox lunged at the squirrel. The squirrel knew in seconds he would be dead. But he felt nothing— no pain, no snapping jaws.

The squirrel opened his eyes to find the brilliant sun shining down on the forest.

The friendly chirps of birds like church bells greeted his ears. Surprised, and relaxing a bit, the squirrel looked around. The dazzling creek was now more crystalline than ever before. The glorious day told the squirrel that it had all been a dream. Though his nightmare could come true, the delighted squirrel knew that it would never happen to him, especially not today.

The Prairie Boy and the Wild Mustangs

Michelle Gooch, 10

H OOVES THRASHED, and dust from the Wisconsin prairie flew up wildly as the black stallion, leader of a wild herd of mustangs, kicked and bit, wildly trying to fend off an intruder.

The prairie boy sat in his crouched position, watching intensely. He hoped for the black stallion to win and felt a confidence that he would, for the stallion's herd could fend off any intruder.

The boy had no name that he could remember, for he had accidentally been left behind on the prairie while his family had been heading for Oregon in a train of covered wagons. He had been three years old at the time and miraculously managed to survive on the prairie for nine years. Now he was a member of the wild mustang herd and ran as free as the wind with them.

By and by, the intruder was chased away, and the prairie boy, barefoot and dressed in rags he had learned to make from buffalo skins, crawled out of his hiding place. The stallion nuzzled him gently, telling him that the battle had been won and showing his pride of winning it.

The boy's only possessions were his bow and ten arrows he had found at a deserted Indian camp. He did not need anything more, for he was part of the wild herd and survived the way they did.

He walked along as the stallion led his herd to a water hole to drink. The prairie boy leaned over, put his lips to the cool water, and drank thirstily.

The herd roamed the prairie for days and days, and soon they came upon wire fences and knew that this was a human ranch and not to go any further.

The stallion quickly led them away from the ranch, but it was too late. A wild scream filled the air, and seven cowboys on tamed horses galloped out, waving lassos in the air. The prairie boy leapt onto the stallion's back, and the herd took off, galloping away from the cowboys. They were chased for many days and nights, and along the way many exhausted mares and their fillies and colts dropped to the ground, unable to go any further, and were caught by the ranchers. After a while, the cowboys began to notice that the horses were running in a large circle and posted new cowboys on fresh horses to intercept them. As the chase wore on, thirst and fatigue overcame the herd, and by the second week of running, the stallion, the boy, and five mares were the only ones left. As three more days passed, the cowboys roped the remaining herd, and a mean and wild cowboy grabbed the boy around the neck.

"Whatcha doin' with the horses, boy?" he yelled, and

threw the boy onto his saddle and walked the exhausted and famished mustangs back to the ranch.

The horses were kept in a small corral, and the ranchers took the boy into their house and tried to get some information out of him.

They asked him questions, such as "Why were you running with the horses?" and "Where is your family?"

The boy, however, could not speak from living with the wild herd for so many years and just sat there, speechless.

"Answer me, boy!" they would always yell, but then Hannah, the rancher's wife, would calm them and say, "Leave him alone. He's only a child," and offer him some of her cornbread.

When the rancher locked the prairie boy in a guest room, the boy screamed and yelled and kicked the walls in a frenzy of terror, for he had not been brought up as a boy but as a mustang. Locking him up in a room would have been like locking up a wild mustang in a small pen.

The rancher and his wife were so confused and horror-stricken that they threw the boy out and yelled, "Go away from here and never come back!"

The boy took off, running like the wind, the breeze whipping through his long hair. He rolled over in the damp grass and gobbled up some berries. Then he ran down to a stream and caught a few trout. He skinned them and ate them raw, and when he had begun to get back the feeling of being free again, he walked back to the ranch, knowing he must save his mustang family.

He unlatched the corral gate, and the entire herd streamed out, hooves pounding like rain. Then they all jumped and pranced away, with the joy of being wild again. The rancher and his wife watched from their window.

"That darned boy," said the rancher. "He's let the mustangs out!"

But his wife pressed her hand firmly on his shoulder and said, "Let them be, for the boy is really a mustang in disguise. The herd could never be captured, nor could the boy. They are as free as the wind and the great blue sky."

And so it was. The boy lived with the mustangs forever more. This was the way it was meant to be for all of them, living their lives in harmony and freedom with the wind and sky.

My Epiphany

Dara Hochman, 12

M Y SWEET BUNNY, HANNIE, lay in my mom's chair. As I
passed by Dad's bedroom that night, I knew it would
be the last one Hannie and I spent together. There was no
reason for knowing that. I just knew it. Hannie had been
sick for a long while. We never knew why she got sick, but
we refused to give up. We took her to many veterinarians
who specialized in exotic pets, since Hannie was a French
lop rabbit. They didn't know what was wrong with her
either, but they recommended different medicines which my
parents had been giving to her every day for the last one-
and-one-half years.

I loved Hannie a lot. She lay there peacefully now. She
couldn't move her legs any more. We had to hold her up
because she was paralyzed. I had spent all day with her,
doing my homework as she rested by my side. Sometimes I

would feed her alfalfa hay and she would give me a kiss with her wet nose.

I got scared that last day when I fed her a carrot. She was choking on it and I was afraid she was going to die right then. But she didn't die. The carrot was in her mouth and my mom reached in and took it out. She told me not to worry when I cried and said that I thought I had killed her.

That was a long day. When night came, I didn't want to go to sleep, but my mother made me brush my teeth and go to bed. I wanted to go in and be with Hannie again before I went to sleep, but my mom wouldn't let me. As I lay in bed, I worried that I would never see Hannie again. I saw her little black-and-white face before my eyes and I knew she loved me. I had asked her to stay until Christmas and she did. Now it was December 30, and I saw that Hannie was suffering a lot since she was so sick. I whispered to her that I would understand if she had to leave, but I didn't want her to ever leave me. I cried until I went to sleep.

The next morning when I woke up my mom was hanging up my clothes. My dad came in and looked very sad. His eyes were teary and red. I knew then that my sweet bunny had left the world and me behind. I said, "Hannie died, didn't she?" Mom didn't say anything, and Dad sat down on my bed and began to cry. I never saw him cry before. He used to wake up in the middle of the night and hold up Hannie and feed her so she wouldn't starve. He cleaned out her cage every day and would talk to her. I knew he loved her very much, too. My mother did also. She was crying.

For the first few minutes of that awakening, I did not cry. I just put the covers over my head and tilted my head up to the ceiling. I prayed it was not true. I prayed so hard.

But the feeling of hurt that my bunny had left me and that emptiness inside of me did not leave.

Love was the power that brought Hannie and me together, but death was the power pushing us apart. It was in the midst of that terrible pain that I realized that Hannie had only left me for a short while. I knew that she would have to come back to me some way. My mom and I talked about it. She said it was like when my grandmother died. My mother was very sad. My grandmother played the piano beautifully. She said I remind her of her mother when I play the piano beautifully, too.

I knew Hannie was out there somewhere but that she wouldn't be a French lop rabbit again because that caused us too much pain. Somehow, I decided Hannie was a little kitty. Mom and Dad went looking all over for a kitty, but it was January and kittens were not born in the winter. They found one kitten out on Long Island, but the woman decided at the last minute not to give it up. I was feeling pretty depressed, but I knew that I would find Hannie again.

February was peaceful. Snow was falling. Children were playing. Something was in the air.

Then, one day in February my mom picked me up and said, "There's an ad in the newspaper for a litter of kittens. The woman wants to find a home for them because she is handicapped and she can't look after them. Do you want to go and see them?"

I said, "Sure," so that night my dad drove us to Nanuet. When we got there I spotted a little tiger kitty lying on the couch. He was just six weeks old. I sat down and petted him. I immediately fell in love with him and when I called him my pet name for Hannie, he seemed to like it. That name was Muffin.

We took Muffin home and as soon as we got there, he sat up on his little rear legs and bent his front paws the same way Hannie did. A friend of ours said, "That's funny, I never saw a kitten do that." I knew in my heart that Hannie was back again. My mom and dad smiled at me. They had tears of happiness in their eyes now, especially my mom. My mother gave me a hug. "She's back, eh?" she said to me, not expecting an answer.

The Ice Hound

Margaret Loescher, 12

THE WIND BLEW, rattling the windowpanes of the cottage in the Welsh mountains. The snow hurtled itself at the small cottage as I sat on the windowsill wrapped in a blanket, staring out into the fierce blizzard. I thought how beautiful and peaceful snow had always been in my life and how I always looked forward to the snow-covered mountains glistening in the cold winter sun. But now that peaceful snow had turned into this menacing, life-threatening blizzard.

It had come on so suddenly that nobody was prepared. I had just finished making breakfast for Grandpa and me and I had used the last of the food except for some steaming soup I had made for Grandpa because he was ill in bed. I was very worried about him because his bronchitis had turned into pneumonia and he was running a fever. There was no electricity or telephone. The wires had disappeared into a snowdrift long ago. And not even a snowplow could get through the narrow country road. I knew I would have to get help somehow. But how could I—a fourteen-year-old boy with only two long skinny legs to carry me?

I rose and let the blanket fall to the floor. I stooped under the low doorway into Grandpa's room.

"Grandpa, there's no food left and I'm worried. I've decided to go to the Half Moon Pub by the priory ruins for help," I said.

"You are very brave, boyo," said Grandpa, raising his hand toward me. I took the shaking hand and held it tight in my own. Grandpa coughed and I could hear his chest rattle and his breath wheeze.

"I'll give you some advice on how to go," rasped Grandpa. "Don't try to travel in the valley bottom for the snow will be deepest there. Take the high pony-trekking path along the side of Loxige Tump. The higher you go, boyo, the less snow there will be." He coughed and his chest heaved. "The wind will have blown the snow off the hillsides and down into the valley."

"I see, Grandpa."

"And there's one more important thing." Grandpa was nearly whispering now. "If you meet a dog, don't be afraid. Follow him."

"What?" I asked, wondering if Grandpa was out of his mind with fever.

"There is a legend in these Welsh mountains that," he coughed heavily and took a long time to get back his breath, "there is an Ice Hound who has saved people," he coughed again, "in danger in the snow." Grandpa fell back onto the pillow and I waited for him to continue the story. "Llanthony Priory fell into ruins after all the monks died in a terrible blizzard." Grandpa coughed weakly. "They all starved to death, and since then the Ice Hound has been seen prowling the valley in snowstorms." It took him a long time to finish and he was very tired.

I thought not to bother Grandpa any longer and so I said, "See you at suppertime!" But deep down in my soul I knew that I very well might not make it or not make it in time for Grandpa.

"Good luck, boyo!" Grandpa breathed as I finished piling more wood onto the fire and slipped out of the tiny bedroom.

I put on my winter clothing. Then courageously I opened the door into the howling blizzard and onto my dangerous journey ahead.

The wind blew wildly at my frozen face as I plodded slowly across the sheep field. When I reached the stream I grabbed hold of a hawthorn tree, gasping for a warm breath. I walked beside the stream, looking down at it. Parts of it were frozen over with a thin layer of ice. The fast-moving parts of the stream still rushed by, carrying huge plates of ice and smashing them on rocks like cracking a china plate on the edge of the sink. I stood at the end of the bridge and placed my foot warily on its frozen surface.

A great gust of wind whirled the snow in clouds around me, and when I could see again, there before me, filling the space at the other end of the bridge, was what could only be the Ice Hound. It was covered with a lot of dull gray fur and had ears like a fox. The eyes were balls of yellow light. I got the feeling that the dog was not solid like any other dog of his description. He looked more like a figure of air. Then a low sound came from the dog's being. I stumbled backward, startled. I stepped back off the bridge and slipped. I started falling down the steep bank and stopped suddenly. I had been caught by a root sticking out of the bank. I felt the root flex under my weight and I knew it wouldn't hold me for long. If I fell into the freezing water below, I would have no chance. I searched wildly for anything to hold onto but there was nothing. Suddenly, something gripped me tightly by the collar and raised me up into the air. Cold breath blew against my neck. I was sat on the bank. I turned around, anxious to see who had saved my life. There, towering in front of me, was the Ice Hound, his ghostly figure huge and his fur blowing in the fierce wind and snow. My grandpa's words came back to me: "If you meet a dog, don't be afraid. Follow him."

I rose and held my hand out to the Ice Hound in greeting and touched his thick coat. A shiver ran through my body for the dog was as cold as the day itself. The Ice Hound took off at a steady pace across the bridge and started along the narrow pony-trekking path. I followed. The path was steep and slippery and I knew that if it weren't for the Ice Hound I would have been well and truly gone— buried in the blizzard.

We climbed higher and higher. The higher we got the less snow there was but the more wind there was, too. The snow was only ankle deep now, but a huge gust of freezing wind blew me off my feet. I lay there in the snow so tired I felt like forgetting everything and going to sleep. Then I felt an ice-cold tongue against my cheek. I got up again and we began to descend.

Suddenly, out of the curtain of snow rose the pointed arches of the priory ruins. They were just a field away. The Ice Hound whined and urged me to hurry. It was as if the great hound was anxious to get to the priory—as if someone or something was beckoning him. So I tried to hurry. I fell

exhausted against the stone wall surrounding the ruins. How would I ever get my weak body over the wall? My limbs ached with cold. Suddenly I felt a furry body heave me over onto the other side of the wall. Then the Ice Hound took a tremendous leap over the wall, his yellow eyes gleaming.

To get to the pub, we had to walk through the priory ruins. The towering stone walls stood high above me, icy and haunting. There was a faint noise and out of the falling snow in front of me appeared a man. He was dressed in long monk's robes. A hood hid his face. He looked like the Ice Hound—as if he wasn't solid but a ghost. Another man just like the first walked right past me and I touched him. He was as cold as the snow but the strange thing was that the figure was really there because I could feel him. Perhaps, I thought, they are the monks of the old priory who died in the blizzard centuries ago. Why didn't I think it was strange for people so long dead to appear now?

We walked on, passing more monks. One of them stopped, patted the dog, and said something to him that I didn't understand. Perhaps it was in Old English or Latin. Gradually I became aware of soft chanting that became louder and louder. A procession of these ghostly monks approached slowly from behind one of the tall walls of the ruined priory. They were escorting a figure that was not robed. As this figure came out of the group and approached me, I gasped, realizing who it was. "Grandpa!"

"Well, boyo, I've come to tell you that you don't have to hurry home." He smiled his old smile and I hadn't seen him looking so well for a long time.

"Grandpa!" I shouted again. I reached for him and fell.

"Get up, boyo! You're almost there!" urged Grandpa.

Once again the Ice Hound took me by the collar, but

with more force, and put me on my feet. I squinted into the snowstorm, searching for my grandpa, but there was nothing in sight except for the ruins.

The Ice Hound whined once again and when I turned to look at him, there was the faint glow of paraffin lamps in the pub windows. I felt desperately sad that my grandpa had died but relieved that I had reached safety. It took all the energy I had to get to the door of the pub.

On the doorstep I turned and looked back at the huge Ice Hound standing alone in the haunted ruins. His yellow eyes were gleaming—the only light in the gathering gloom. I owed him my life. The Ice Hound threw back his head and howled a mournful cry. A sudden gust of wind and snow blew between us, and when it settled again there was no sign of the Ice Hound, but the howl hung in the wind.

A Ride with Fate

Robert Brittany, 12

Billy woke up in a cold sweat. His pillow was wet. He got out of bed and hobbled to the window. His leg was still hurting him from the accident. Billy looked out the window and remembered. He remembered it well.

Twelve-year-old Billy McCall lives down the road from Mr. David Reed. Mr. Reed is seventy-one; old, but healthy and strong. The ninety-nine acres that Mr. Reed owns was once a dairy farm but is now where he boards horses for their owners. Mr. Reed takes care of thirteen horses. His horse, Buck, is the strongest, and is the leader of them all. No wonder; Buck is a Tennessee Walker thoroughbred. Mr. Reed enjoys riding Buck. In the summer Mr. Reed would ride Buck almost every day. In winter when the grass is usually covered with a couple of feet of snow, Mr. Reed would give the horses hay, but Buck would get hay and oats. Every week Buck was groomed, and once a month his hooves were cleaned.

Billy was walking up to Mr. Reed's farm to ask him if he could ride Buck. If he could, this would be the twelfth time. Billy could only go on weekends, so he had to finish all his homework before he went. Billy didn't like to walk on the road. He didn't like the paved roads, the cars, the electric fences or the TV antennas on every roof. Billy didn't like any of these things. You could do without them, he thought. So instead, Billy walked through the field that joined Mr. Reed's property with his.

It was two o'clock Saturday afternoon, and there wasn't a cloud in the sky. Billy saw Mr. Reed as he was finishing painting the fence that led from the barnyard to the pasture.

"Hi, Mr. Reed. Are you enjoying this summer weather we're having?"

"Yeah, I am, Billy. By six o'clock tonight this paint will be as dry as a horse's throat without water. I guess you want to take Buck out, right, Billy?"

"Yeah, I do. It's a nice day, and I've got all my homework done, too."

"OK. He's in the first stable. I'm going to wash this brush and go inside. When you come back give Buck some corn. You know where it is."

"Don't worry, Mr. Reed, I will."

Billy got Buck out of the first stable and tied him to the part of the fence that was already dry. Before Billy went to the saddle shed, which was next to the first stable outside the barnyard, he stopped and looked at Buck. He saw his brown hair gleaming in the summer sun. He saw Buck's broad chest, his strong muscular thighs, and his mane blowing free with the wind. Billy got the saddle and put it on him. The other horses in the barnyard talked to each other, probably about what they will do, and where they will go when Buck is ridden away, Billy thought. Billy fastened the girth under Buck's stomach, adjusted the stirrups, and got on. He rode Buck down the lane and onto the road. Billy was always careful with Buck while riding along the narrow country highway, because he knew Buck was one of a kind.

Billy rode Buck along the road for about a half hour and then decided to turn off of it. He rode through a field that was once a thriving dairy farm in the late eighteen-hundreds. The land was rich and fertile. No one owned it now, but somebody was supposed to buy it in October.

Billy led Buck down to the creek and let him drink. He saw the sun setting and knew he had to get home, but fast! Billy leaped on Buck, kicked his ribs and yanked the reins. Buck took off like a shot. He galloped all the way to the road and then slowed down to a trot. Billy remembered when Buck started to gallop, his powerful legs pushing off the ground, heaving his body forward and then thrusting himself forward again.

When Billy got back to Mr. Reed's farm, he unsaddled Buck, put the saddle away, led Buck into the barnyard, and gave him some corn.

After he gave Buck his corn, Buck walked down to the creek in Mr. Reed's field, and all of the other horses followed. They wanted to be with their leader; they wanted someone to follow.

That Thursday in school Billy got a social studies test back. The teacher put it on his desk face down. Billy could see all of the red marks through the back. He turned the test over and looked at the grade. His eyes bulged, his heart started beating faster, and sweat started pouring down his face. Billy's first urge was to rip it up, but he knew he couldn't. He slipped the test in his folder and looked around the classroom like nothing was bothering him, but he still had a dazed look in his eyes the whole day.

That weekend Billy finished his homework and walked over to Mr. Reed's farm. It was a beautiful Saturday, just the right weather to ride a horse: bright, sunny and a small breeze.

When Billy got to the farm, Mr. Reed's blue Chevy pickup was gone. Billy thought he went to get horse feed or hay. He knew Mr. Reed wouldn't mind if he rode Buck. So Billy got Buck out of the stable and saddled him up. He got on Buck and rode down the gravel lane.

At the end of the lane Billy looked down the road to see if any cars were coming. When Billy turned his head to the left, he caught a glimpse of his house. He remembered what his father said to him when he showed him his test. He couldn't understand why his dad told him that this would be his last time riding Buck. Billy's riding Buck didn't even affect his grade on the test, and Billy knew it.

As horse and rider rode along the black-topped road, Billy decided to go to the Stone Edge Quarry, because this was the last time he could ride Buck. The quarry trail was a nice, long, quiet and peaceful ride. Billy's father worked at the quarry, and Billy was thinking about him, so that probably helped him make up his mind.

Finally Billy got to the quarry's gate. Well, it wasn't really a gate, it was just a chain that was stretched across the entrance, about three feet above the ground.

As Billy pulled back on the reins to stop Buck, he saw the signs near the entrance. KEEP OUT; NO TRESPASSING; OFF LIMITS ON WEEKENDS; CLOSED TODAY.

Billy got off Buck and unsnapped the chain from the big white post, took hold of Buck's reins, and walked over the chain. He fastened the chain and got on Buck.

As Billy rode the horse through the quarry, he thought of his father again. It got him so mad that he couldn't ride Buck anymore. Why, he thought to himself, why. He studied hard for the test, but he just froze up when it was given to him.

Billy was startled when he thought he heard a dog's bark in the distance ahead. He heard it again. It seemed to be getting closer!

Suddenly, a big black German shepherd came flying around the bend.

"Oh, no!" Billy yelled. Buck, seeing the big dark hairy animal and hearing Billy's terrifying cry, was alarmed so much that he pushed off the ground with his hooves and started to gallop toward the chain.

Buck was out of control, and Billy couldn't do anything to slow him down.

Where did the dog come from? It might have been a stray, or it could have been the quarry's guard dog, but there was no time to guess where some dog came from. Buck was getting closer to the chain! Billy knew Buck could jump it. The dog was still behind them, barking, howling and running faster than ever. There were stones laid on top of the quarry road, so pot holes wouldn't come up so soon. The chain was getting closer. Billy knew Buck could jump it, he had to.

"Come on, Buck, old boy. You can do it," Billy said as Buck was still running full speed, and as they were about ten yards away from the chain. Five yards . . . four yards . . . five feet.

"Jump!" Billy screamed as Buck pushed off the loose stones with all fours.

"Neigh," grunted Buck as his two hind hooves scraped the chain. Then another painful grunt as his legs hit the ground. Buck kept on running as long as he could, which was only about fifteen yards away from the quarry's entrance. By then Billy had gotten him under control. The dog had disappeared somewhere on the quarry road, but Billy didn't know where he had gone.

Billy hopped off Buck and looked at his legs. The front ones were fine, but when he looked at the hind ones, his eyes bulged, his heart started beating faster, and sweat started pouring down his face just like when he got his test in school. Billy grabbed the reins and started to walk with Buck. He didn't get on Buck, because his hind legs were already very swollen, and getting on his back would only make them worse.

The worried boy and the horse walked up the lane to the barn. If Mr. Reed was there, what would he tell him?

As Billy came to the back of the barn, he saw Mr. Reed's Chevy. A desperate kind of fear swept through him as he was frantically searching for words to tell Mr. Reed. He wanted to let Buck loose in the field as fast as he could, so he unsaddled him, put some cream on his hind legs, even though there was no cut, and then led him into the barn-yard. As Billy shut the gate to the barnyard, he heard foot-steps behind him.

"How was the ride, Billy?" asked a cheery voice behind him. "Where did you go?" Billy turned around with an expression that Mr. Reed recognized immediately. Holding back the tears, Billy tried to explain.

"Well, Mr. Reed, I . . . uh . . . well, I went to the quarry,

and we were riding along when all of a sudden I heard a dog's bark and that's . . ."

"Don't finish. Where's Buck?" Mr. Reed asked Billy in a quick and concerned tone.

"I put him in his stable," the shaken boy answered as Mr. Reed opened the red painted stable door and went in. Billy stayed outside and waited for Mr. Reed to come out. In about five minutes he came out and looked at Billy.

"I can understand why you didn't obey the signs. Nobody does, because there's only rocks to steal, but there's a lot more in that quarry than what they dig up."

"Yeah," Billy said with a grin that lasted about three seconds.

"As for that dog," Mr. Reed said as he paced in front of the guilty-looking boy, "I don't know where it came from, but in all my years of riding horses, I never went to that quarry. Why, there are already sinkholes and snakes, and now on top of that, stray dogs."

"I'm sorry, Mr. Reed. It won't happen again," Billy said, trying to hold back the tears.

"I know it won't happen again, and it's not going to. That's why I don't want you to ride . . ." Billy's head dropped.

"Just don't tell my parents what happened. This is supposed to be my last time riding."

"All right, I won't," Mr. Reed said as Billy started to walk home through the field.

One week had passed, and Billy didn't go near Mr. Reed's farm or Buck.

In school he was getting grades like A and A-minus, especially in social studies. One day after school Billy had a talk with his father.

"Son, you've been getting A's in school, and your social studies teacher tells me that you are doing great, so I've decided to let you ride Buck any time on weekends you want." Billy smiled. He had to, or his parents would think something was up.

"Wow! That's great, Dad," Billy said as he tried to look as happy as he possibly could.

That Saturday after dinner, Billy went to his room to get a baseball and glove. While he was in his room he looked out of the window and saw something going down Mr. Reed's lane. It looked like a car. It was a car. It was Mr. Reed's Chevy. Why throw a baseball around when you can ride a horse. It's been five weeks, and Mr. Reed was sure to have cooled down by now, Billy thought to himself. So he told his dad he was going to ride Buck and that he'll be back in about half an hour. As Billy walked through the field he asked himself why he couldn't ride Buck. It was just an accident that that dog scared Buck. It wasn't his fault.

When he got to Mr. Reed's farm, the Chevy wasn't there, so he got Buck out of the barnyard and saddled him up.

"How ya been, Buck? I'm just going to ride you down to the road today," said Billy in his happiest voice.

"Say, Buck, do you remember when I took you to that field that was once a dairy farm. Boy, when you started to gallop. Wow! You really took off."

When he stopped thinking about Buck, he realized that he was about five yards away from the lane and in the middle of the road.

"Where are you trying to take me, boy?" Billy turned Buck around on the road but stopped to look at the sun. It was almost setting, too. What a picture! Billy turned around to see if any cars were coming.

"No!" S C R E E C H! Car brakes slammed.

"Neigh!" Buck fell down with a thud, and Billy with him. Mr. Reed got out of his blue Chevy.

"Oh my God, Billy!"

The gleaming sunset lit up the evening sky, and in the distance you could hear a faint gunshot coming from Mr. Reed's barn.

Dance of the Gazelles

Sarah Thomson, 12

K ATIA LOOKED OUT AT THE WORLD in which her ship had crashed and sighed. It was so ugly! Well, maybe ugly was not the right word. Harsh, bleak, forbidding, awesome. Those were better.

The ground was red—a dull, dusty red. How ironic that red had always been her favorite color. She ought to get tired of it by the end of this trip, but she wasn't now, not yet anyway. Huge pikes of rock, also red, pointed like fingers to the sky. Remnants of an ancient civilization, she remembered having been told. They didn't look it.

Katia mentally shook herself. This will get you nowhere, Katia, she told herself firmly, sitting here thinking about people who are dead. You'll be dead if you don't go do something!

She carefully rose out of the seat, ducking her head so that she wouldn't hit it on the low ceiling. Why, oh why,

couldn't they make ceilings tall enough for normal human beings? It shouldn't be hard to make at least a few ships two inches taller. But no, "You just don't understand the practical side of life, Katia." Her lips curled in distaste as she mimicked the supply monitor, Morl. Well, this should be a good test of her practicality.

She tapped impatiently on the "Door Open" button. The panel slid open and she slipped outside. The blast of heat hit her like a towering wave hits a swimmer, drowning her. She gasped. The two days of sitting inside the ship, looking out and waiting, had not prepared her for this searing, intense heat. She mopped the sweat that was running freely down her forehead and looked towards her forest. Ah, there it was. Not a large forest, but where there were trees, there was water. And where there was water, she could live. She shook her head, sending droplets of sweat flying, and went back into her ship.

Katia sighed in relief as she closed the door on the blistering heat and was once more in the air-conditioned place. She stood for a moment, allowing the manufactured coolness to seep into her bones before hurrying to collect what she might need.

She had consumed all the drink in the tiny space vessel and for this she cursed herself. Oh well, nothing she could do about it now. Something to cover her head from the sun...there was only the seat. She rummaged for a knife among the various compartments; but she hesitated a moment before cutting the material. It seemed almost like sacrilege...she and the ship had been through so much together. "Don't be silly, Katia," she told herself. She must be overexcited. Carefully she plunged the knife into the seat.

Clouds of stuffing rose. Kati stopped to wave it away

from her face. It almost seemed as though the chair were trying to get back at her. "Kati, stop it!" she said aloud and got a mouthful of stuffing. She spit it out and resumed her job. When she left for her forest, she had a large piece of cloth and a knife. To survive with.

To walk across the desert was torture. The sun beat down on her like giant hammers, pounding on her bowed shoulders, beating her into the ground. Slowly her mind seemed to grow numb. Her legs moved automatically, carrying her forward. Sometimes she wondered hazily if she was going insane, but more often she didn't think. Thinking brought awareness and awareness brought the pain . . .

She didn't even know she was in her forest until the sunlight was blocked off. She looked up and saw the leafy fronds above her and collapsed on the lush ground to sleep the dreamlessness of exhaustion.

When she awoke, her first awareness was of being horribly thirsty. She staggered upright, gripping the rough limb of a tree for support, and peered about her for a water source. There was none; no, wait. That at the end of the little clearing—what was it? Her unclear eyes focused on a small trickle of blue and she walked unsteadily towards it. It was a stream. She bent to drink, then stopped. Through her trained mind flashed the firmly imprinted warning about water: never drink water you don't know about! It might be contaminated, radioactive . . . but natural instinct overcame these. She knelt and drank. It was delicious.

Katia straightened up, flinging wet strands of brown hair back from her face. She felt refreshed, wonderful, ready to try anything. It was when she was walking back to where she had dropped her knife that she realized she was not alone.

The young girl forced herself to go through the useless,

pointless motions of picking up the knife and putting it in her belt, although she didn't know why, before turning to face her companion.

It was a gazelle.

Katia sighed in relief. A gazelle. A simple, brown-eyed, shy, harmless thing. Yet ... there was something different about this animal. Was she mistaken, or was there a look of intelligence in its melting eyes? And why did it stand there so quietly, watching her?

"Who are you?" The question was out before she thought about it. "You're insane, Katia Darnet, talking to an animal!" she scolded herself.

But the gazelle answered.

Well, perhaps answered was not the right way to put it. Rather, it responded. It spoke directly into her mind.

"I'm of the Mytaughs. We are an ancient race of beings who once lived in the ruins on the plains. But we were not a good people. There was anger and hatred, greed and jealousy. A small group of us left and came into the forest, where we discovered the beauty of song and the joy of dance and the goodness of living simply. The rest of our civilization died out; but we remained. We now call ourselves the Aions."

"Why are you telling me this?" Katia's question was spoken aloud.

"We think you may be one of us."

This is crazy, Katia thought. I should be running away, screaming. Instead she stood up, extending a hand to the gazelle.

"Show me your dance."

The gazelle led her back to the open plains. There was a group of gazelles standing in the sun, poised as though waiting for a signal. Her guide ran to join them, but still they did not move until, at no signal she could see, they burst into a wild, joyous dance.

Their dance was as intricate as a spider's web, as lovely as dew sparkling on that airy creation. They danced for the joy of it, for the love of creating something beautiful. Katia was caught up in the rhythm of it; her spirit flying skyward on the wings of an eagle to plummet suddenly downward and crash on the sun-baked ground when the dance stopped.

When she saw why, her spirits fell even farther. It was a spaceship hovering above her and coming down to the earth.

They were coming to take her home.

The gazelles moved towards her, sensing a creature in anguish, longing to comfort. Their presence gave Katia the strength to hold her head high to meet her fate squarely. She knew what her answer would be.

The spaceship had landed and Morl had stepped out. He glanced nervously at the gazelles. Poor thing, could he not see their beauty? Did his blighted mind recognize only what might be a threat to himself?

"Katia?" his voice was uncertain. "I've . . . I've come to take you home."

"I'm not going." Katia's voice rang out clear and proud. "I'm not going."

"What?!?!" Morl's face was pale, his jaw working soundlessly.

"You heard me, Morl. Go back. Go back to the world you're used to. This is my world and I'm staying here."

Morl stared at her a minute, flabbergasted. Then he turned, shaking his head, and went into the ship. The engine started, the thing rose out of sight and the dance resumed.

Katia hesitated a moment, then flung herself into the wild, joyous dance of the gazelles.

The Wyoming Wildness

Jeffrey Ryseff, 12

Twenty years ago this summer, I attempted to go on a journey with my dog.

I woke up just before the rooster crowed. My eyes were watering as I opened them to the bright sun. My mother, a tall woman with dirty-blond hair, usually wore the same dress, a worn-out yellow dress that went right down to her toes. She was making breakfast, for I could smell the eggs and ham. My dad was probably getting an early start in the fields.

As I was putting on my clothes, I thought of something I missed very much. My dog, Ole, was a black Lab. He ran away from home two years ago on my birthday.

That day I turned twelve, but it wasn't a very happy birthday, even though my mom tried hard to please me.

I was fourteen on this day, another birthday. I have light brown hair and stand about five-foot-two.

I used to wear the same overalls for a year until I got a

new pair for my birthday. There was really nothing to look forward to.

I put on my clothes and walked out of my room. My mom was making breakfast.

"Hi, honey," she said.

"Good morning," I replied in a sleepy voice.

I sat down and started munching on my eggs.

I barely finished my eggs when I heard a bark. It was a familiar bark. I got up and practically ran through our screen door. My mom said it was probably just one of the wild dogs, but I knew it wasn't just any dog.

There was a black glare coming from the left field of white corn. I knew it was him. I started running, and he ran faster. I ran into him and he practically knocked me down. My heart was in joy like kids at play. I was going to watch him all night so he couldn't run off again.

I brought him in our house and gave him some liver that was left over in the refrigerator. I knew this was going to be my best birthday ever! I practically gave him five bowls of liver. That's how I knew he had not eaten in weeks.

He started whining. I knew something had to be wrong. I let him outside and he was looking at the left side of a mountain about seven miles away.

That night I looked down at Ole and he was lying wide awake. I started to wonder if there was really something up there on the mountain. My heart told me to go and the rest of me told me to go too.

I woke up at dark and packed for my journey even though I didn't know what was going to happen. I packed ten egg sandwiches and ten bags of liver. I brought a pocket knife and some rope. I was on my way.

I was about fifty feet from my home and walking at a

brisk pace. My dog was eager and happy because I had decided to go.

When it started to get light, I could see little animals hopping and skipping around. Trees were turning lighter and lighter as the early morning went by. Before I knew it, it was midday.

At lunchtime I had a half of one of my sandwiches. As I was munching on the last bit of the sandwich, I saw a roll of Ace bandages. I picked it up and put it in my sack.

Twenty minutes later I was back on my way. My dog was leading me by about ten paces.

I was probably one mile from the top of the mountain when Ole started acting up, like a hound losing its coon. I could tell by the tone of his voice that there was some enemy around. Out from behind a strangely shaped rock came a mountain lion threatening me. That was when my dog stepped in. He attacked the lion and bit his neck, not letting go. I knew my dog had won. He let go and walked toward me with blood running from his teeth. I was proud of my dog's killing.

It was just about dark, so I set up camp and fell asleep.

Bright and early, I was awakened by my dog as he licked my face. I looked up at the bright sun and saw hawks flying overhead nearby. I packed up my stuff and walked to where the hawks were. I was behind a large rock about four feet high and eight feet long. I crept behind the rock and saw a man lying flat on his back. I ran over and checked to see if he was breathing. He was breathing a little and was bleeding badly. I was glad that I had found a roll of Ace bandages on the way.

While I was wrapping the bloody leg, I found a mountain lion's tooth in his leg. I slipped it in my pocket.

That night I kept him warm and my dog lay right by his side.

I knew that was why my dog wanted me to go up to the mountain. This was probably his owner after he ran away from me.

I woke up early in the morning and the man was recovering. He was up hugging Ole. My heart went low when I knew I had to let him go.

The man said thank you and walked away with Ole.

"Where are you going with him?" I said in a sad but loud voice.

"This here dog's mine," he said.

"Well, let's see who he wants to go with," I said.

Ole just stood there between the man and me. He crept over slowly toward the man. And then he ran to me and jumped all over me!

My dog and I went home with smiles on our faces. I was so happy that I could cry.

I never saw that man again, but I remember his face as my dog and I went off in the distance.

The Bear

Lena Boesser-Koschmann, 11

THE MORNING WAS COOL. It wasn't cold, but not warm enough to go without a jacket. Sandy and I were walking toward the field where Chipper, my seven-year-old pony, was staked. I was swinging the reins, and Sandy was walking beside me. We didn't talk to each other, and it was quiet. A bird chirped, singing out a strange melody. When we arrived, I softly called to Chipper. He lifted his head and walked slowly over to me. He nuzzled my pocket to see if I had any treats for him. I laughed and slipped the bit into his mouth. He jerked his head a little at the coldness of the bit. I unhooked the rope from his halter and, grabbing the reins in my hand, jumped up onto his back. Since Sandy was taking the road, I decided to canter Chipper in the field.

As I neared the road that separates Chipper's field and Timer's field (Timer is Chipper's brother), I noticed a guest from the Goldhill Inn. He was taking a video of the inn. He nodded a friendly hello to me, and I decided to show off a little. Maybe he'd videotape me. I clicked Chipper again and gave him a little kick. He loped faster. When he came to the edge of the field where Timer was staked, I stopped him and let him walk.

Timer was going crazy. He was running around in circles, bucking and kicking his legs. I thought his unusual behavior was just in his excitement to see Chipper. I let Chipper walk up to him, and Timer kicked him. Timer was acting really weird. It was then that I noticed the bear. He was sitting in the berry patch no more than sixty yards away. I gasped. Chipper jumped. Quickly, I leapt off Chipper and tried to pull him away from Timer. It was impossible.

Just then Sandy called, "What's wrong?"

"Bear." I spoke that one simple word.

"What?"

"Bear," I repeated.

"Where?"

"In the berry patch, right over there!" I pointed over toward the raspberries that were around one side of the garden. I was talking fast and calmly to Chipper, pulling at his head a little at a time. Finally, we were walking away from Timer, who was as wild as ever.

All the time I have had Chipper, I have never actually come within sight of a bear while riding (unless you count the time I heard snuffling in the woods and saw fresh droppings). Chipper was getting excited by now. He was hard to control from the ground. I ran him to the nearest tree and tied him quickly to it. It was only then that I relaxed and looked closely at the bear. It wasn't a big bear, but I'm not too good at telling what age animals are. Maybe he was the one-year-old that had been hanging around the town.

"He's so cute," I said to Sandy, who was looking at the small bear also.

"I know. That might be the one we saw in our yard the other day."

Just then Mrs. Hall shouted out her window at us, "There's a bear right there, ya know!"

"We know," I shouted back and then untied the reins and started walking back toward my house.

Once we were out on the road, I leapt up onto Chipper once again.

"What are you doing?" Sandy asked.

"I'm going to put Chipper back in the pasture. Then we can come back to see the bear some more."

"Thank you for your permission, oh great one," she said.

I giggled. Then I loped Chipper down the short pathway to our house. He seemed to know where we were going. He automatically went to the gate of the big pasture. I opened the gate and he trotted inside. I slipped off his reins, and he loped across the pasture to scratch on a stake. Then I ran to tell my mom about the bear.

When I reached the porch, I didn't bother to use the steps—I never did—but vaulted up onto the porch.

When I opened the door, Carrie, my sister, greeted me with a questioning look.

"I thought you were going riding," my mom said.

"We were, but the horses are all hyped up because there's a bear in Mrs. Hall's berry patch," I answered.

And at the same time Sandy said, "There's a bear over at Mrs. Hall's."

I laughed. "I think it's the same one that was in our yard the other day," I said. "Sandy and I are going over to see what it does."

"Well, Carrie and I are going down to the school in about fifteen minutes. I have some work I need to do before tomorrow. Tell me about the bear when I get back."

"Sure."

Then Sandy and I walked back across the road to Mrs. Hall's place. She was yelling and screaming and banging pans at the bear.

"She's mad," I said matter-of-factly.

"Very good," Sandy said sarcastically.

"I can't see the bear," I said, standing on my toes and trying to see it.

"Let's go over where we were before." But we didn't get a chance to because just then we saw Bill slowly walking, gun in hand, toward the bear.

"No!" I gasped. Why would anyone shoot a baby bear? A bear without its mother. A bear with nowhere to go. Bill aimed. Then a shot rang out.

"God," Sandy said, obviously mad. I couldn't speak. I was boiling over with anger—a steam pot that can't stop boiling, even when the burner beneath it is off. Maybe it wasn't dead. Maybe he had just shot to scare it. Then why had he aimed the gun? I argued with myself. "I am never speaking to him again," I said under my breath.

"What?"

"Nothing. I just feel sorry for the bear."

"I know. I mean, it couldn't defend itself. They didn't have to shoot it," Sandy said in a sarcastic voice.

"No kidding!"

Then, we walked wordlessly back toward my house. Mom and Carrie were just leaving. They had these looks on their faces. They had heard the gunshot, obviously. "It's dead." My voice cracked as I said it.

"Who shot it?" my mom asked.

"Bill Hall." Sandy spoke his name in disgust. Just then we saw Mrs. Hall walking toward the Jones' place, her kids hanging on her.

"Is it dead?" my mom called to Mrs. Hall, even though she knew the answer.

"Yes," Mrs. Hall called back matter-of-factly.

"Why did you shoot it?"

"I didn't shoot it, Bill did!"

Great, Mrs. Hall, blame it on Bill. Mrs. Hall went on, "You know what happened yesterday? He was growling at me from behind the woodpile." Then Silvie started crying, and Mrs. Hall continued walking.

All my mom said was, "Come on, Carrie, let's go." And they rode off.

I slowly walked over to Chipper. He looked at me with his big brown eyes and yawned. I forced a smile. "He's dead, Chipper, dead." And I buried my face in his strong neck.

Mountain Seer

Clea Paine, 10

I T WAS THE MIDDLE OF JANUARY, on a cold and frosty morning in my field, and it was early. In fact, the sun had begun its journey across the sky not long ago, perhaps five minutes or so. It was marvelously clear and crisp and I was up and about in a minute, full of unused energy. Sunlight was streaming through my window which I had made out of a broken piece of glass I found around my old home in the suburbs. The bright day seemed to reach in and grab me as I was unsnarling my fur, for I was out in the splendor of morning before I had time to know I was going there.

I was intimate with my field. I knew every rock, every nook and hiding place, every route over every brook, I knew everything there was to know about my field. I even knew how many lichens there were on my favorite rocks.

Surrounding my field you could find almost anything.

On one side there were mountains and lush green pine woods. On the other side there was a slim fast-flowing river with many small fish. Beyond was a cliff with a waterfall that contributed to the river. And finally, at the far end was a huge, deep, cool lake, providing a home for trout, minnows, water bugs, and assorted species of pond weed.

Beyond the lake and through a few feet of thick trees and undergrowth lay the biggest mushroom patch you've ever seen. It had every species of mushroom you can imagine, from big fat boletes to lacy coral mushrooms, from gray mushrooms to toadstools, they all grew there. On every surrounding tree grew thousands of shelf mushrooms. This was my favorite eating spot, my marvelous mushroom patch.

The one defect and flaw of my field was that it was the perfect place for coyotes who lived on the mountainside to hunt. They had to travel through only one mile of undergrowth to get here. The river gave them something to drink and a small snack of fish, and if they were in the mood for a bigger meal they could always go to the lake and catch some trout or catfish or a mouse like me in the field. The lower parts of the cliffs were a good place for their kids to play and so was the field. They always loved to chew on mushrooms in the mushroom patch. They'd usually come down about once a month and stay a few days at the edge of the woods where all the other mice lived.

On this particular morning I was walking by the side of the river when I saw fresh coyote tracks. I began to feel panicky and headed back in the direction of my house, always hugging the ground. I began hearing coyote footsteps behind me and I started to run. The footsteps began to run, too. I forgot about staying low or being unnoticed; I forgot about everything and began a life-and-death dash towards safety.

The footsteps were close behind me as I ran with the short stubs of dead grass whipping me. I felt a pain in my sides, but I kept going for what seemed like forever until finally, far ahead, I saw a woven grass door standing open, the door to safety. I began to slow so I could get in without skidding and heard again the running footsteps. I prepared to turn and jump, and jump I did. I turned in mid-air and closed the door behind me as I glided the last few feet to the ground.

The next thing I knew I was in bed at dusk. I must have slept all day. I heard coyotes slinking around. They had woken from their daily sleep to hunt again. I made it through this time, but being a mouse is tricky.

Voice of the Gray Wolf

Kelly Brdicka, 9

I MAGINE, ONE STARRY EVENING you are looking out your bedroom window at your home in a snow-covered Canadian forest. You look up, up to the vast azure sky full of beautiful twinkling silver stars. Their soft, silver light floats through the window, calling you, changing you . . .

Until you feel yourself running, running swiftly through the snow with your pack. You have long, white fangs that glisten in the starlight and a small, black nose that can smell prey a mile and a half away. Your two thick fur coats keep you warm, even in the twenty-below-zero climate. You are a female Alpha gray wolf, hurrying home to the den in the mountainside, where your pups are waiting for you.

As you enter the den chamber, your pups whine and stumble up to you. Tomorrow will be their first day on a hunt. Stumbling down beside them, you fall asleep with the pups. The next morning is calm and the sun spreads its rosy-golden glow on the smooth, white snow. The adults awaken early and perform their chorus howl, a beautiful untamed music that bounces off the looming mountains as loud and as clear as a ringing church bell.

The pups come out of the hidden den entrance in the rock, listening and joining in with their small puppy howls. They sound like little mice! The adults all change notes after a breath and start howling again, a different, wild music that drifts through the thick, dense forest like the wind. The adult wolves stop howling and you sniff the air. A familiar scent comes to you. Moose! You start to run, your head held high, a proud, dominant leader, and the pack, your mate, and your pups follow. The hunt is on!

As you move toward a large meadow, a hawk cries nearby. It circles and heads straight for one of the pups. You and your mate growl and howl, showing your long fangs. The hawk circles low around your head. You claw and snarl. The hawk cries in pain and flies away into the clouds. You move on, scenting the lost trail of moose once again.

You pass a glistening frozen river as you run toward the moose, your goal. After many hours, you reach a large clearing, and there it is, the moose. It is young and weak. The pack loses no time closing in and making the kill. Even the pups feast on the large beast.

When everyone has eaten their fill, they start back to the den, tired and full, as dusk sets in, leaving the foxes and ravens to eat their fill of the leftover carcass. Your pack stops and laps up cool snow for a drink on the way home.

As you come in sight of the den, you raise your head to

howl. But as you do, you look up, up to the vast azure sky full of blinking, silver stars. Their lovely, silver light falls on your fur, calling you, changing you...

You are sitting on the window seat of your bedroom window, gazing up at the twinkling, silver stars, just like the gray wolf as she throws back her head and howls that untamed music through his forest home in Canada.

Security

Jessie Eyer, 11

The house is brightly lit,
but yet something is still missing.
The cheery noises of the house,
the clattering of dishes.
A cold, blank feeling jolts your stomach,
as the door to your room slowly starts to open,
But it is only the cat.
The soft, thick, velvet warm fur,
the low, smooth, thick, silky purr
and those clever blue eyes
watching over you,
nuzzling its wet nose against you,
as you hold it in your arms.
A warm, soft feeling
comes into your stomach
leaving the cold one to the never-ending night,
and know that everything will be all right.

FROM THE EDITORS OF
STONE SOUP MAGAZINE

The best place to find more writing like the stories in this book is in our magazine, *Stone Soup*. We started *Stone Soup* in 1973, when we were nineteen years old. The magazine began as a college project and became a lifelong project! *Stone Soup* was an immediate success, and now, so many years later, it is the leading magazine of its kind in the world.

We invite you to become a regular *Stone Soup* reader. The magazine is published every two months and can be found in many bookstores, as well as in school and public libraries. You can find us at www.stonesoup.com on the internet.

We also invite you to become a *Stone Soup* contributor. Wherever you live, if you are under the age of fourteen, you are invited to send us your work. The stories in this collection give you a good idea of the quality of the work we are looking for, but in our magazine we publish stories on every subject, not just animals. Stories may be any length. If you want a response from us, you must enclose a self-addressed stamped envelope. Send submissions to:

Ms. Gerry Mandel
Stone Soup
P.O. Box 83
Santa Cruz, CA 95063
USA

To order *Stone Soup* for your home, school, or library, use our Web site, or, if you live in the United States or Canada, call us toll-free at 800 447-4569. From other countries we may be reached by telephone at 408 426-5557 or by fax at 408 426-1161. *Stone Soup* is published in Santa Cruz, California.

We look forward to welcoming you into the *Stone Soup* family of readers and writers. Perhaps one day a story of yours will appear in *Stone Soup,* or even in one of our future anthologies.

—The Editors

Look for *The Stone Soup Book of Friendship Stories* at your local bookstore or online at www.tenspeed.com.

ABOUT THE
CONTRIBUTORS

Because these pieces were selected from twenty-five years of *Stone Soup,* the authors are now many different ages. Some are adults, some will be graduating from high school soon, and some are still young enough to publish more writing in *Stone Soup.* We were able to find out what most of our contributors have been doing since their work first appeared in *Stone Soup.*

Lena Boesser-Koschmann

Lena's story "The Bear" was based on the true experience of witnessing the death of a baby bear in the rural Alaskan town where she grew up. The experience was traumatic, she says, but it also helped lead her to the path she is taking now—studying and working with the relationships between animals and humans as an environmental studies/environmental politics major. She plans on going into environmental law, and her favorite animal will always be her black pony Lupine, whom she received as a gift on her seventh birthday.

Kelly Brdicka

Kelly wrote "The Voice of the Gray Wolf" as a school project. She likes reading (especially fantasies), and also enjoys swimming and playing dolls. Kelly urges others to respect animals' natural habitats, and to take good care of their pets. She has three siblings, and her favorite animal is a dog named Max.

Robert Brittany

Robert's story, "A Ride with Fate," was inspired by the summers he spent on his grandparents' farm. He writes, "Animals have always been the greatest teachers to me. They demonstrate a sense of ever-forgiving love and constant devotion even to those who don't love them as well as they should." Robert graduated from the Widener University School of Law in 1997, but stresses that "you don't need to be a lawyer to have a positive impact on shaping the laws that affect animals or the world that animals live in."

Jessica Eyer

Jessica wrote "Security" at a time in her life when she felt very lonely and her cat Clumpy comforted her. She wants people to realize that animals have feelings too, and that we should treat them well. Jessica, who still writes, also loves creating music. She aspires to be a music and movement therapist.

Colleen Flanagan

Colleen, now a senior in high school, worked last summer as a veterinary technician at an animal hospital, where she reaffirmed her decision to become a veterinarian. She writes, "Animals have a simple purity and an honesty that draws us to them." Some of Colleen's favorite authors are Edgar

Allan Poe, Emily Dickinson, Elizabeth Barrett Browning, and Robert Jordan.

Michelle Gooch

Michelle's story, "The Prairie Boy and the Wild Mustangs," was inspired by her fascination with wild horses. Riding horses is her main interest, and she competes in the fields of combined training-dressage, cross-country, and show jumping. Michelle writes, "Animals offer loyalty, charm, and a type of unconditional love." She urges people to have their pets spayed or neutered to help prevent overpopulation.

Dara Hochman

Dara's story, "My Epiphany," was inspired by the passing on of her French lop rabbit. Now a student at Bryn Mawr College, she writes poetry and plays, and enjoys reading, painting furniture, and being involved in the theater. She plans on going into a career related to media or the arts. Her favorite animals are her cat Muffin and his cat-friend Omi.

Kathi Hudson

Kathi, a full-time mom to three boys, also has eight books to her credit (seven on public education and one on Christian parenting). She feels that animals can be instrumental in healing, through the love and encouragement they bring to people's lives. Evelyn Ross, Kathi's grandmother, submitted Kathi's story "Coon Wolves" to *Stone Soup* when Kathi was twelve. Kathi dedicates this story to her grandmother, and thanks her for starting her in her writing career.

Andrea Johnson

Andrea is now studying to be a forensic anthropologist at San Diego Mesa College. Her story, "Athena's Gold," grew out of her love of llamas and the mountains. She enjoys hiking, music, studying, and reading (Tim O'Brien and C. S. Lewis are some of her favorite authors). She believes that we should stop hunting animals, destroying their natural habitats, and using them in scientific research.

Jessica Limbacher

Jessica's writing has been published in *Stone Soup, New Moon, Children's Magazine, Acorn, Word Dance,* and *Young Voices.* She enjoys reading the Harry Potter series, Robert Cormier, Jerry Spinelli, and J. R. R. Tolkien. She says, "This is the first story I've ever had published in a book, and I'd like to dedicate it to my dog and two cats—some of the best friends you could ever have!" She plans to be a doctor and writer when she is older.

Margaret Loescher

Although Margaret wrote "The Ice Hound" while she was living in England, the story is set in Wales, which she often visited as a child. Her family moved frequently when she was young, and she feels that taking care of her pets in new environments helped her settle into new places more quickly. She is beginning her master's degree in visual anthropology at Manchester University, and plans on becoming an ethnographic/documentary filmmaker.

Clea Paine

Clea, who wrote "Mountain Seer" for extra credit when she was in elementary school, is currently studying archeology at Tufts University. Clea enjoys reading French literature and Terry Pratchett novels, and still writes from time to time. She wants people to preserve open spaces for wild animals.

Leah Rosenblum

Leah wrote "Age, Dust, and Animals" for a creative writing class. She would like to thank her writing teacher, Ms. Turketsky, for encouraging her to submit the story to *Stone Soup*. Currently working at a public relations firm, Leah plans on becoming a librarian. She enjoys water polo, swimming, hiking, biking, fishing, spending time with her family, and reading. Some of her favorite authors are Steinbeck, Martin Amis, and Plato.

Jeffrey Ryseff

Jeffrey's tale was inspired by the book *Where the Red Fern Grows*. Currently he is a senior at Arizona State University, and is majoring in business. He plans on going into advertising or marketing, and enjoys snowboarding, camping, fishing, and reading articles and short stories. His favorite animals are horses and his memorable dog Buffy.

Daniel Whang

Daniel, a junior at Duke University, wants to pursue a career in either investment banking or management consulting. He enjoys playing golf, tennis, and volleyball, and expressing himself through music and visual art. His favorite thing to read is the *Wall Street Journal*.